Classic Christmas

Tales

CONTENTS

The Night
Before Christmas

Illustrated by Jenny Press, courtesy of
Simon Girling & Associates

The Night Before Christmas

'Twas the night before Christmas when all
through the house
Not a creature was stirring, not even a mouse.
The stockings were hung by the chimney with
care,
In hopes that St Nicholas soon would be there.
The children were nestled all snug in their beds,
While visions of sugarplums danced in their
heads.
And Mama in her 'kerchief, and I in my cap,
Had just settled down for a long winter's nap;

When out on the lawn there arose such a
     clatter,
I sprang from my bed to see what was the
     matter.
Away to the window I flew like a flash,
Tore open the shutter and threw up the sash.
The moon, on the breast of the new-fallen
     snow
Gave a lustre of midday to objects below,
When what to my wondering eyes should
     appear,
But a miniature sleigh and eight tiny reindeer.

With a little, old driver so lively and quick,
I knew in a moment it must be St Nick.
More rapid than eagles, his coursers they came,
And he whistled and shouted and called them
by name:

"Now, Dasher! Now, Dancer! Now, Prancer and
Vixen!
On, Comet! On, Cupid! On, Donner and
Blitzen!
To the top of the porch! To the top of the wall!
Now, dash away! Dash Away! Dash away all!"

As dry leaves that before the wild hurricane
     fly,
When they meet with an obstacle, mount to
     the sky,
So up to the housetop the coursers they flew,
With the sleigh full of toys, and St Nicholas
     too.
And then, in a twinkling, I heard on the roof
The prancing and pawing of each little hoof.
As I drew in my head and was turning around,
Down the chimney St Nicholas came with a
     bound.

He was dressed all in fur from his head to his
     foot,
And his clothes were all tarnished with ashes
     and soot.
A bundle of toys he had flung on his back,
And he looked like a pedlar just opening his
     pack.
His eyes – how they twinkled! His dimples –
     how merry!
His cheeks were like roses, his nose like a
     cherry.
His droll little mouth was drawn up like a bow
And the beard on his chin was as white as the
     snow.

He had a broad face and a little, round belly
That shook when he laughed like a bowlful of
    jelly.

He was chubby and plump, a right jolly old elf,
And I laughed when I saw him in spite of
    myself.
A wink of his eye and a twist of his head
Soon gave me to know I had nothing to dread.

He spoke not a word, but went straight to his
    work,
And filled all the stockings; then turned with a
    jerk,
And laying his finger aside of his nose,
And giving a nod, up the chimney he rose.
He sprang to his sleigh, to his team gave a
    whistle
And away they all flew like the down of a
    thistle.
But I heard him exclaim, ere he drove out of
    sight,
"Happy Christmas to all and to all a good
    night!"

The Little Angel
with Silver Hair

Illustrated by Jenny Press, courtesy of
Simon Girling & Associates

The Little Angel with Silver Hair

Once upon a time there was a little angel with beautiful, silver hair. She had been naughty and Saint Peter sent for her.

"Come here, naughty one," he said. "You do not seem to realise that everyone here in Heaven has work to do, especially at Christmas time. We all have to make someone on Earth happy."

She hung her head and Saint Peter frowned and said,

"But **you** have been lazy and can no longer stay with us. So, off you go — you must go down to Earth and make someone happy. Until you do, you will not be allowed back to Heaven!"

So the little angel found herself outside the gates of Heaven wondering what to do. Down to Earth she flew and found everything covered in a blanket of snow. She was very cold in her thin clothes.

"Good afternoon," called out a rabbit as it hopped by leaving deep pawprints.

Suddenly there was the sound of sleigh-bells and into view came Santa Claus.

"Hello, little angel, and what are you doing on Earth?"

She hung her head in shame and confessed she had been lazy and naughty in Heaven.

"Well, come and do some work for me," said Santa. "Hop on the sleigh and I'll tuck you in."

After a while Santa stopped the sleigh and chose some splendid, green Christmas trees. Then he emptied out of his sack tinsel, toys and Christmas decorations.

"Would you like to help me decorate these Christmas trees?" he said.

"Oh, yes please!" said the little angel with a big smile.

"Good," said Santa. "I'll do the tops and you can decorate lower down."

They set to work and soon all the tinsel and toys were used up. Santa went to get some bigger presents and promised to collect her on his return.

The little angel suddenly noticed that one little tree had no decorations. Whatever could she do?

Suddenly she had a good idea. There were shining, golden stars on her dress and she took them off and hung them on the branches. What else could she use? Oh yes! Strands of her beautiful hair. She draped these round the tree and it looked really lovely when she had finished. Even the deer came to admire it.

When Santa came back he said,

"That was a very loving thought," and patted her kindly on the head. "Now, we must take these trees to the nearest village and perhaps you can find someone to whom you can take your little tree."

So Santa and the little angel went on the sleigh across the snow until they saw the lights of the next village twinkling in the distance. They stopped in the centre and Santa delivered all his presents.

The little angel did all she could to help until at last the time came for her to deliver the Christmas tree decorated with her shining, golden stars and her silver hair.

She carried the tree to a house where three good children lived. They were helping their mother to wash up as the angel tip-toed into the house and left the lovely tree as well as some presents.

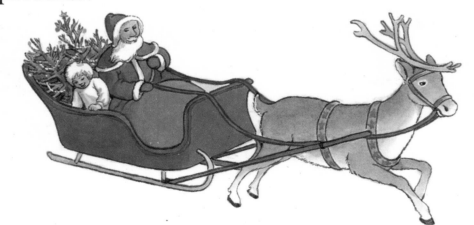

She peeped through the window as the children danced with delight when they saw the tree and presents.

"Isn't it lovely! Somebody very kind has left all this for us."

The little angel smiled happily and ran to join Santa in the sleigh.

"Now where do you want me to take you?" Santa asked.

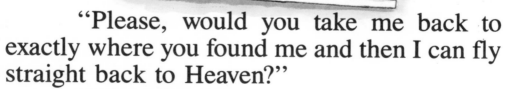

"Please, would you take me back to exactly where you found me and then I can fly straight back to Heaven?"

"Right," said Santa, setting off. "Thank you for all your help and I'll make sure Saint Peter hears about it."

"Thank you and goodbye," called the little angel as she flew off.

When the little angel arrived back at Heaven Saint Peter was waiting.

"**Now** what have you been doing?" he asked. "Just look at your hair and where are your golden stars?"

When the little angel told him what had happened to her hair and her stars, however, Saint Peter was very pleased with her and said,

"Now you can come back into Heaven."

He was so pleased with the little angel that he gave her some more golden stars and the older angels stitched them on to her robe for her.

As for her lovely, silver hair . . . well, that will grow again!

The First Christmas

Illustrated by Jenny Press, courtesy of
Simon Girling & Associates

The First Christmas

Long ago, in the town of Nazareth, there lived a beautiful and good young woman, named Mary, who was to be married to a carpenter, named Joseph.

One day an angel appeared to Mary. He greeted her and told her not to be afraid and said,

"You will bear a son and will call Him Jesus. He will be a holy child, the Son of God."

Some time after the angel's visit, it was decreed by the rulers of the land that everyone had to return to their own town to be taxed and, as Joseph came from Bethlehem, he and his wife, Mary, had to travel there.

Joseph and Mary were poor so Joseph walked while Mary rode their donkey.

It was a long journey and when they arrived in the town they were tired and in need of a place to sleep but Bethlehem was so crowded with all the people who had come to be taxed that they could find no place to stay.

At last they stopped at an inn and Joseph asked if they could stay there for everywhere else was full and Mary, his wife, was so tired that she could travel no further.

"I'm sorry," said the innkeeper, "but, you see, the town is full and there is no room in the inn."

"Is there nowhere we can stay?" asked Joseph sadly as he held the tired donkey's reins.

"Well," said the man, "there's always the stable, I suppose. It's not much but at least it's warm and dry for your wife."

Mary smiled her thanks and she and Joseph made their way to the warm stable where the innkeeper's donkey and oxen were quietly munching hay.

Joseph made a comfortable bed for Mary in the hay and straw that lay on the floor and during the night the Baby Jesus was born. Mary wrapped Him up warmly and laid Him in the soft hay of the manger.

The donkeys and the oxen watched as He lay smiling up at His Mother, Mary.

In the fields around Bethlehem there were shepherds watching over their sheep and protecting them from thieves and wild animals. Suddenly the darkness of night was gone and a bright light shone all around them.

An angel appeared in the middle of the light and said to the terrified shepherds,

"Do not be afraid for I bring you joyful news. Tonight in Bethlehem is born a baby who is Christ the Lord. Glory to God in the Highest and on earth Peace and Goodwill to all men."

The frightened shepherds clung together as the angel disappeared and the glorious light faded from the night sky and then one, braver than the others, said,

"Let us go down into Bethlehem and see if we can find out what has happened."

So all the shepherds made their way into Bethlehem and found the stable where the Baby Jesus lay in the manger with the animals watching Him.

They found the baby and His Mother and bowed down and worshipped Him. They left a lamb as a present for Him and went back to their fields rejoicing.

Three Wise Men from the East who had studied the heavens followed a star for many weeks because they believed it foretold the birth of a King and Saviour. They went first to King Herod for they thought the birth would be at his court but he knew nothing and asked them to return with news of the baby when they had found Him.

They followed the star further until it seemed to stand still in the sky, right over the stable where the Baby Jesus lay.

The three Wise Men went into the humble stable and kneeling before Baby Jesus and His Mother gave Him gifts of gold and frankincense and myrrh.

When the Wise Men left they were warned by God in a dream not to return to tell King Herod where the Baby Jesus was for he wanted to harm Him so they returned to their own country by another way.

Joseph was also warned in a dream of the danger so he took Mary, his wife, and the Baby Jesus and fled into Egypt where King Herod could not find them.

That is the story of the First Christmas, the birth of Jesus, which happened two – thousand years ago and is still celebrated today.

The Christmas Workshop

Illustrated by Jenny Press, courtesy of
Simon Girling & Associates

The Christmas Workshop

In the autumn, when the leaves are falling and the days are becoming shorter, you may see lots of stars twinkling at night. You may even see one special star, shining a little more than the rest. Well, inside that special, bright star is the Christmas Workshop where clever fairies work.

Throughout the year, winter, spring, summer or autumn, the fairies will be hard at work there making all kinds of things — toys, clothes, cakes, dolls and teddy bears. Imagine any toy you like . . . the fairies can make it. That is why they are known as the 'clever fairies'.

These fairies (who are really tiny angels who wear white dresses) gather together on every night of the year, except, of course, Christmas Eve itself, to work in the Christmas Workshop. In the autumn, however, they work even harder to get ready for Christmas.

This is the room where all the dolls' clothes are made. One fairy cuts the cloth to the right size and passes it to another fairy who sews it on a sewing machine. Another fairy sews by hand and yet another puts on pretty ribbons.

When all the clothes are made yet more fairies dress the dolls in their new clothes.

Now we are in the very heart of the Christmas Workshop where all the toys are made. Most of the toys are made from wood and the fairies are busy shaping, cutting, sawing and fitting pieces together to make lots of different sorts of toys.

They make dolls' houses, toy trains with trucks, sledges, toy cars, skis, rocking horses, tiny Christmas trees, Noah's Arks full of toy animals, farmyards with cows, horses, pigs, sheep, geese, ducks and hens, spinning tops, puppets and many more.

When all these toys are finished yet more fairies paint them in bright and cheerful colours.

You can almost taste the mouth-watering smells coming from the next room . . . and no wonder, for that is the Christmas Workshop Bakery where all the fairy chefs work.

One fairy beats egg whites with a whisk for meringues; another rolls out the pastry which her friend cuts into different shapes with the pastry-cutter; yet another mixes a big bowl of icing.

Across the room is the oven where the scones, tarts and other goodies have been cooking. One fairy is sprinkling caster sugar on some currant buns. Perhaps the luckiest fairy of all is the one who tastes the food to check all is well.

This is the room where the cleverest of the clever fairies work. Have you ever wondered what happens to all those toys that children break and then throw away? Well, the clever fairies collect as many as they can because with care, skill and patience they can repair them and make them as good as new.

If a leg is missing from a doll they make another. If a furry rabbit has lost one of its ears they make another and sew it on.

It is just the same with teddy bears or toy trains. The clever fairies will rescue them and repair them.

Iam sure that by now you have guessed the reason for all the work that goes on round the year at the Christmas Workshop. It is to make sure that Santa Claus never runs out of presents. Every year the clever fairies make thousands of lovely toys for boys and girls of all ages.

Then, on Christmas Eve, Santa Claus arrives with his sleigh, pulled by his six reindeer, and parks it on a cloud, just outside the Workshop. All the fairies help him to load his sleigh with sackfuls of presents ready for his magic journey on Christmas Eve.

Some clever fairies help Santa Claus with his tasks so they, too, fly down to Earth on their little, fairy wings.

Just outside the Christmas Workshop they have planted Christmas trees and on Christmas Eve they deck them with candles, coloured lights, bells and Christmas stars. Then, with a few presents for some lucky children tucked under their arms, the fairies fly off with their decorated Christmas trees – down to Earth.

Did you enjoy your peep into the Christmas Workshop? Next time you play with your toys you might just wonder if **they** were made in the Christmas Workshop.

Perhaps they were . . .

Rudi, the Little Reindeer

Written by Maggie Kay
Illustrated by John Geering

Rudi, the Little Reindeer

Rudi, the little reindeer, stood by the door watching his mummy and daddy set off.

"You be a good deer for Auntie Ruth!" called Mummy.

"We'll be back soon," Daddy cried, "and next year, you'll be big enough to help us."

Rudi waved goodbye then he heard Auntie Ruth say, "Come in now, Rudi. You'll get chilled there."

Rudi did not care. He wished he could be one of the reindeer chosen to pull Santa's sleigh. Mummy and Daddy had told him all about it. It sounded so exciting to fly over the roof-tops – magical, even!

Auntie Ruth gave Rudi some warm milk and read him a bedtime story when he was tucked up in bed. But Rudi could not stop thinking about pulling Santa's sleigh.

"I wonder where Mummy and Daddy are now?" he murmured. "Perhaps they're flying right over my head!"

Rudi tiptoed to the window and looked out. The sky was black – no moon, no stars, nothing! The little reindeer was disappointed. He went back to bed but he could not sleep.

After a while, Rudi decided to go downstairs for a drink of water. He peeped around the sitting room door and saw Auntie Ruth fast asleep in an armchair in front of the television.

As Rudi crept through the kitchen, a bright blaze of light shot past the window.

"Wow!" gasped Rudi. "What was that?"

A trail of silver stars floated down from a white streak left in the sky.

"Santa's sleigh!" thought Rudi. "It must be!"

The little reindeer could not help himself. He silently crept out of the kitchen door and into the garden. He was a funny sight in his pyjamas.

Rudi could see the white streak disappearing into the distance. He started to run …

"Santa will have to stop soon to deliver presents," Rudi was thinking aloud. "If I catch up with him he'll have to let me help. He can't send me home."

Rudi ran on eagerly … for miles … and miles … and miles …

"Oh, I'm out of puff!" he suddenly realised and he stopped to catch his breath.

When he looked up into the sky, ready to follow the trail again, it had vanished. The sky was dark.

Rudi looked around but the only light he saw came from the white snow on the trees that surrounded him. The little reindeer felt afraid.

"Which way did I come?" he wondered.

Then, gladly, he saw his hoofprints in the snow.

"That way!" he laughed. "My own prints will show me the way home."

Sad to have missed Santa but glad to know his way home, Rudi trudged through the snow. Soon he grew weary.

"I'll just have a little nap under this tree," he yawned, "then be on my way once more."

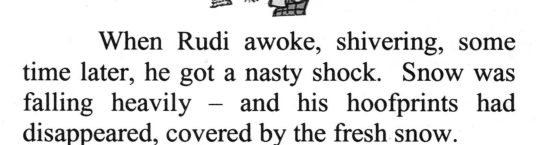

When Rudi awoke, shivering, some time later, he got a nasty shock. Snow was falling heavily – and his hoofprints had disappeared, covered by the fresh snow.

"I'm lost!" he sobbed, and a tear ran down his cheek. "What a silly deer I've been. I should have stayed at home – just as Mummy and Daddy said. Now I may never see them again."

Ting! A noise made Rudi look up just then.

A golden star shone brightly on the ground before him. As Rudi stepped towards it, the star leapt away. Ting! Rudi moved closer and, again, the star took off, making Rudi follow.

"Are you a guiding star?" asked Rudi, and the star twinkled brighter as if in reply. "Can you lead me home, please?" the little deer asked next.

The star sparkled and glowed, then almost bounced across the snowy ground. Rudi bounded along behind.

After a while, Rudi spotted a picnic area that he had visited with his mummy and daddy. He knew he would soon be home.

"I'm so lucky to have found you, golden star," Rudi sighed happily.

Just then, he saw lanterns up ahead. Voices shouted. They were calling, "Rudi! Rudi!"

Rudi's heart leapt with joy. It was his mummy and daddy searching for him.

"Mummy! Daddy! I'm here!" Rudi whooped with excitement.

In no time, his parents were hugging him.

"Thank goodness you're safe!" Mummy cried.

"Thank my lucky star!" smiled Rudi, and he told his parents all about it.

From then on, Rudi knew he would always be safe with his lucky star looking after him.

A Christmas Carol

Illustrated by John Geering

A Christmas Carol

Ebenezer Scrooge was an old miser. He would not spend a penny on heating his office. He made his assistant, Bob Cratchit, work in the freezing cold. Bob would have loved to leave his job but he needed the little money Scrooge paid him to support his wife and children.

Christmas was coming and Bob thought of his youngest child, Tiny Tim, who was lame and walked with a crutch. He knew that he could not afford to buy his poor son even the smallest present. When Bob brought up the subject of Christmas, all Scrooge would say was,

"Christmas? Bah, humbug!"

That evening, as Ebenezer Scrooge sat by his flickering fire, he heard a frightful clanking and rattling and the ghost of his dead business partner, Jacob Marley, appeared. Marley was bound in chains, made of cash boxes and bags of coins, which weighed him down and rattled as he walked. Scrooge was terribly afraid.

"Change your ways," said the ghost, "or you will end up like me. Tonight you will be visited by three Spirits. Heed them well."

Marley's ghost had spoken the truth.

Later that night, as the clock struck midnight, the first of the three Spirits appeared.

"I am the Spirit of Christmas Past," she said. "I will show you all that has been."

The Spirit took the trembling Scrooge from his bed and flew with him into his past life. She showed him all the terrible things he had done and all the people to whom he had been unkind because of his greed and love of money and who now cursed his name.

The second Spirit was a jolly, round gentleman who carried a glowing torch.

"I am the Spirit of Christmas Present," he said. "Hold on to my robe."

Scrooge held on to the Spirit's robe and was carried away, through the night, to the house of Bob Cratchit. Bob and his wife sat at the table with Tiny Tim and their other children. Scrooge paid his assistant so little that it was a very poor meal, yet Bob held up his glass and said,

"Here's to Mr Scrooge. May he have a Merry Christmas."

The old miser bowed his head in shame.

"Take me away from here, Spirit," he said.

The third Spirit was a terrible, hooded spectre.

"I am the Spirit of Christmas Future," he said. "I will show you things that have yet to be."

Again Scrooge was taken to Bob Cratchit's house and again it was Christmas but there was no mirth and no jollity. There was an empty seat at the table and a small pair of crutches hung on the wall.

"No! No!" cried Scrooge and sobbed bitterly as he watched Bob and his wife and children wipe away their tears.

The spirit said,

"This may indeed come to pass but need not be."

Then the Spirit took Scrooge to a churchyard and pointed to an overgrown and neglected tombstone on which was carved a name.

EBENEZER SCROOGE

"No, Spirit! No!" cried Scrooge. "Take me back to my bed. I will change my ways. I swear I will."

The Spirit did as he was asked and when Scrooge awoke the next morning he remembered all that he had learned from the three Spirits.

It was Christmas morning and Scrooge jumped out of bed with a big smile on his face. He dressed hurriedly and rushed out into the street, throwing pennies to small beggar boys and wishing everyone as he passed,

"A Merry Christmas! A Very Very Merry Christmas!"

Scrooge went into the shops and bought as many presents as he could carry and took them all to Bob Cratchit's house. He gave Bob a large pay rise and declared that he now knew the true meaning of Christmas.

And so, Tiny Tim observed,

"God bless us, every one!"

The Sad Soldier

Written by Maggie Kay
Illustrated by John Geering

The Sad Soldier

The toys lay under the Christmas tree, still wrapped in their Christmas paper, waiting for the children to rush through and find them. Stockings hung by the fireside and a brightly-coloured clown's head appeared from the top of one.

"Is anyone awake?" he asked. "I'm Clive the clown and I'm bored hanging around here."

"I am," squealed a girly voice. "I'm Sandie, a fashion doll."

"Mama," gurgled a baby doll's voice.

"Anyone else?" asked the clown.

"Me," said a quiet voice from another parcel.

"Tell us who you are then."

"Er, Soldier Sam, sir," replied the voice.

"Ooh!" cried Sandie. "You must be very brave."

"No," he said, sighing sadly. "Everyone expects me to be brave but I'm not."

"A soldier who's a scaredy cat?" Clive laughed unkindly but stopped as the children ran in.

"Has he been? Has Santa come?" they cried.

David was first through the door followed by Claire with little Louise tagging along behind clutching her nightie.

"Yes!" cheered David. "Look!"

The three children rushed to open their presents and Clive the clown peeped out so he could see the scaredy-cat soldier.

First David opened his biggest parcel. It was a tank, just right for a toy soldier. Then he found Soldier Sam. Clive watched as David put Sam inside and pressed the remote control button that made the tank zoom round the room.

Just then, Claire took Sandie out of her box. Clive thought she was rather nice but, at that moment, Soldier Sam whizzed past Sandie in his tank. The clown noticed the fashion doll smile at the soldier but Sam's face was growing whiter with fear the faster the tank travelled.

"What a soppy soldier," thought Clive. "Surely Sandie will prefer someone bolder like me."

When all the parcels were opened and Louise had put Baby Doll in a new crib, David looked around the room.

"Our stockings!" he cried, pointing to the three stockings hanging on the wall.

He lifted them down for his little sisters and turned his own upside down. Clive, the roly-poly clown, tumbled out with lots of other goodies.

David looked to see what Clive could do and then he put him aside and went back to play with Soldier Sam and the tank. Clive <u>was</u> annoyed.

"Huh! He'd rather play with his soppy soldier than with me," he thought huffily.

To make matters worse, when the children fell asleep that night, Sandie spent a long time chatting to Soldier Sam and ignored Clive.

Some Christmas crackers lay on the floor and they gave Clive an idea to get Sandie's attention. He jammed one end of each cracker below a table leg and pulled the other. Bang! Crack! Bang!

Sandie squealed and Soldier Sam dived down shouting,

"Take cover! We're under attack!"

Baby Doll began to cry but a loud laugh made her stop. Clive was wobbling with laughter.

"Under attack - from Christmas crackers! Ho, ho, ho! What a soppy soldier you are."

Soldier Sam hung his head in shame but Sandie glared angrily at the clown.

"Your nasty trick scared her," she scolded.

"And Soldier Sam," laughed Clive. "It was just a bit of fun to show you how soppy he is. Not like me - I'm not a scaredy cat."

"You're not nice either. Not like Sam."

Just then the door opened and in padded Jasper, the children's cat. He caught sight of Clive and put out a paw to investigate.

Clive's roly-poly body wobbled and Jasper liked the way it bobbed up and down when he pawed it. He patted Clive more and more.

"Help!" called Clive.

"Who's a scaredy cat now?" teased Sandie. "The cat's just having a bit of fun."

However, Soldier Sam jumped into his tank and drove it towards the cat. Surprised, Jasper let go of Clive and prepared to pounce on Sam.

Although he was shaking in his boots, Soldier Sam headed straight for Jasper. As the cat leapt towards him Sam pressed the remote control button and the tank shot forward at top speed - straight under Jasper who was in mid air. The astonished cat landed with a thud, a dazed expression on his face.

As the cat recovered and fled from the room, Sandie told Sam he'd been very brave. Clive could only agree.

"Thank you for rescuing me, Soldier Sam," he said. "I'm very sorry for the nasty things I said. You may have saved my life."

"My hero," smiled Sandie, hugging Sam.

After that, Soldier Sam was never sad again.

Santa's Weighty Problem

Written and Illustrated
by John Geering

Santa's Weighty Problem

Santa's bathroom scales fell into pieces under his weight as he stood on them to weigh himself.

"I said you were overweight, Fatty," wailed Mrs Santa.

"I wish you wouldn't call me Fatty," said Santa woefully, looking down at the broken scales. "Those scales certainly weren't very strong," he added.

"You are a 'Fatty'. Don't kid yourself. It's all that lazing around you do for the rest of the year," scolded Mrs Santa. "You need more exercise!"

Santa looked down and groaned. All he could see was his large tummy. He could not see his feet even when he breathed in hard.

"Hmmm, maybe I could do with losing some weight," he thought to himself, "or I'll never be able to get down those chimneys."

So he set off for a brisk walk to burn off some of the weight, waved off by his dear wife.

"You'll have to walk around the world several times before you lose that lot," she called after him but a wind was blowing and Santa did not hear her.

He was striding along through the snow, puffing and panting like a steam engine, when he slipped on some ice and the wind caught him. It blew him off balance and down a very long, steep slope.

"Whoops!" shouted Santa and began to roll down the steep hill gathering snow all the way down until he was just an enormous snowball which came to rest at the foot of a tree. Santa's muffled voice began to call out for help.

"Never heard of a talking snowball before," said a big bear, staring suspiciously at the snowball.

"That's not a talking snowball, Bear. Somebody must be trapped in there," said a very clever squirrel. "Let's light a fire to melt it and let them out," he added.

They built a fire and as the snowball melted a very bedraggled Santa appeared.

"I didn't know you delivered presents in a snowball," said the bear scratching his head.

Santa shook off the rest of the snow and looked at his watch.

"Gracious me! Look at the time. I'll be late for delivering all the presents."

"You had better hurry up back up the slope," advised the clever squirrel. "It's a long way up."

Santa braced himself and then started to climb.

"I can't let all those children down," he called back to the clever squirrel and the big bear.

"Thanks for dropping in," called the big bear.

The slope was very, very steep and the snow came over Santa's boots making the journey back up hard, tiring work but, after a while, Santa reached the path at the top and made his way home where his wife was standing waiting for him.

"Goodness me! You've lost a lot of weight!" she exclaimed. "You'll get down the chimneys easily now."

"Give me time to catch my breath and I'll be on my way," gasped Santa with a very red face.

Santa changed into some dry clothes and had a hot chocolate drink before preparing the sleigh and harnessing the reindeer who, by the way, all remarked how young and fit he looked this year - much better than last year.

"She'll not be able to call him 'Fatty' any more," laughed one cheeky reindeer.

Once all the presents were loaded on to the sleigh, Santa set off.

"Not as heavy to pull this year," added the cheeky reindeer.

In fact, without all that extra weight, Santa did his rounds in half the usual time and everyone remarked on it, including the cheeky reindeer.

When he returned, Santa finished his favourite meal - cheese on toast with a slice of tomato and a dash of sauce - and Mrs Santa handed him his Christmas present. He opened it and, when he saw it was an exercise bike, he laughed a hearty laugh.

"What's this? A bike that doesn't go anywhere?"

"It's to keep you fit, my dear," laughed his wife, "so you can help me with the housework. That should keep your weight down."

And do you know - it DID.

The Stable Mouse

Written and Illustrated
by John Geering

The Stable Mouse

Once upon a time, in a land not all that far away, there lived a little mouse. His home was in the corner of a stable and he was very proud of it and kept it neat and tidy and just to his liking.

He awoke one morning feeling bright and cheerful. Although he could not understand why he felt so cheerful, there did seem to be an exciting buzz in the air as if something wonderful was about to happen. After a breakfast of cheese, he swept out his small and cosy room and then peeped out of his front door into the stable itself.

He could see several animals there, eating and gossiping among themselves.

He wondered what they were talking about and stood at the door of his mousehole and listened.

The old, grey donkey and the cow both agreed that something wonderful was indeed about to happen but they had no idea what it would be.

The goat said that he had heard very strong rumours that something was about to happen; something very important but, as he could not be certain exactly what it was, he could not really tell them any more.

The hen stood and flapped her wings excitedly but she, too, did not know what was going to happen and had only heard the same rumours.

The little mouse crept closer so that he could find out what was going on.

However, when the little mouse tried to join in the conversation, the other animals all looked at him in surprise and the horse lowered his head, snorted and said,

"I am afraid we are not interested in your opinion. After all, such a small creature as you couldn't possibly have anything important to say. Go away!"

All the animals turned their backs on the little mouse and he crept sadly back to his tiny house in the corner of the stable.

He was very hurt and lay sobbing on his bed and thought how sad it was that he was too small to be important.

Eventually he fell asleep with the tears still in his eyes.

It was late evening when the little mouse woke up. He stood at the doorway of his mousehole and peeked out.

He decided there was definitely something happening in the stable because all the big animals were quietly excited and jostling for position around the manger in the middle of the stable.

Something wonderful was happening and the little mouse could feel it in his heart, as it leapt with a joy he could not understand.

He ran to the foot of the manger and looked up. It seemed a long way for a tiny mouse to climb but he felt it was important that he should.

The wood of which the manger was made was rough and gave the little mouse a surface for his paws to grip.

Slowly and surely he began to climb towards the top, muttering to himself,

"Up we go . . . up we go," for encouragement, but it seemed an age before he finally arrived at the very top, right in front of the rest of the animals who were also straining to look in the manger.

"Well really," muttered the cow haughtily.

"No manners, some folk!" snorted the horse.

The little mouse looked down into the manger and his eyes lit up with surprise.

For there, in the manger, lay a baby, all snug and warm, fast asleep. It was the most beautiful baby the little mouse had ever seen.

Then the baby opened His eyes and looked at the little mouse and He gave a big smile. The mouse smiled shyly back and nearly fainted with joy.

Then the mouse put his paw into his coat and took out a small piece of cheese and offered it to the baby. A hand from the other side of the manger took the cheese gently from the mouse's paw and the mouse looked up into the face of a beautiful lady who leaned forward and whispered something into his little, silky ear.

From that night onwards, the little mouse was no longer ignored by the rest of the animals.

He was always invited to join in with a meal or a conversation. For the rest of the animals had learned that being bigger than somebody else did not make you more important.

Secretly, of course, they hoped that the little mouse might tell them, one day, what the beautiful lady had whispered to him.

The Adventures of Nina The Angel

Written by Maggie Kay
Illustrated by John Geering

The Adventures of Nina The Angel

Once upon a time all the angels in Heaven were getting everything ready for Christmas. They were baking biscuits and cakes: they were making puddings and sweets: they were wrapping gifts for all the children on Earth.

They were all very busy except for the youngest angel who was called Nina. She just got in everyone's way. To make matters worse, she ate the biscuits just as soon as they came out of the oven.

Nina had such a sweet tooth that she could not resist trying a piece of cake and even sweets too. Well! You can guess what happened. Nina got a terrible tummy ache.

She was helping one of the other angels when her tummy-ache got worse and worse. In the end she had to sit down on a little, fluffy cloud and hold her poor tummy. Great big tears fell from her eyes. Poor Nina!

She was sitting there looking very sorrowful, with a tiny spot of stardust on her nose, when Saint Nicholas found her and took pity on her.

"Well, well, well! What's all this?" he asked in a friendly voice. "You come along with me and I'll give you something for your tummy upset."

So saying, Saint Nicholas took Nina by the hand and led her to a little medicine cupboard in the clouds. There he gave a spoonful of soothing medicine.

Half an hour later, Nina was well enough to go for her music lesson with the other angels. Saint Nicholas was listening to the groups of angels who were singing and playing flutes. Nina joined one of the groups, nearest Saint Nicholas. Soon he began to hear some strange sounds. He put his hand behind his ear so he could hear better.

"Who is making those dreadful noises?" he asked.

Though little Nina was hidden behind the taller angels, Saint Nicholas still found her.

"Sorry, Nina," said Saint Nicholas. "I think you had better not play today. You are making a noise as if your **flute** had tummy-ache. Come back another day and practise."

So poor little Nina, who was feeling rather sad, went and sat on the edge of a cloud listening to the other angels singing and the music was so soothing that she fell asleep.

Moments later, Nina fell off the edge of the cloud! Before she knew what had happened she was falling, falling down to Earth. She was almost down to the ground before she remembered her tiny wings. Fortunately she fluttered them just in time and landed softly in a snowdrift. In the snow-covered distance was a little town.

Now Nina was very curious about Earth and when she saw a bright light shining from a window, she could not resist peeping in. She saw lovely, glowing candles on a Christmas tree and a room filled with toys.

Just then a little boy called Peter walked into the room. At first he did not see Nina at the window. He had just picked up his teddy bear when he saw her.

"Gosh!" he thought. "I must be dreaming!"

Peter rubbed his eyes and Nina vanished into thin air but when he looked at the window-pane he saw it was speckled with stardust from Nina's nose.

That evening, Peter's mother and father took him to the Christmas Eve service at church. On the way to church, Peter saw her again and pointed joyfully.

"Look!" he cried. "It's my angel and there is some golden stardust on the snow!"

"Yes," said his mother patiently. "But now we must hurry along or we will be late for church."

So, with his mother and father, Peter entered the church. He liked to hear the singing and, after prayers, the choir began to sing *Silent Night, Holy Night*.

Then Peter heard a beautiful sound - a silvery voice which he could hear above all the others. He looked around in wonder and there, upon a pillar near the ceiling, he could see the little angel. It was she who was singing so beautifully. Peter smiled at her happily and Nina smiled back.

Late that night, Nina flew back to Heaven. Her visit to Earth had been exciting. She had met Peter and had learned what a nice place the Earth could be when everyone sang praises to God but the best thing she had discovered was that she had a beautiful voice.

"Saint Nicholas **will** be pleased and tomorrow I'll sing my favourite carol for him . . .

'Silent Night, Holy Night.
All is calm, all is bright.' "

Christmas in the Forest

Written by Maggie Kay
Illustrated by John Geering

Christmas in the Forest

It was Christmas Eve. All the rooftops were thickly covered with snow and glittered in the setting sun. Suddenly the sound of sleigh bells was heard in the forest nearby. Could it be Santa Claus? Yes, of course it was Santa Claus - and high time too, for lights were beginning to go on in the houses and children were already waiting, looking hopeful and excited.

Oh dear! Look at the strange trail that Santa Claus was leaving behind him. Nuts and apples, sugar biscuits and sweets lay in the snow where the sleigh had passed by. The little angels had forgotten to mend a hole in Santa's sack.

Along came a little deer and sniffed at one of the biscuits. Soon a fox and a squirrel joined him. Hoppy Hare and Squeaker Mouse had seen what was happening and they came along too.

Before long all the good things had been eaten up and there was nothing left but a pair of slippers lying in the snow. The animals sniffed curiously at them but slippers were no good to any of them.

"Perhaps Goblin will know what to do with them," said Hoppy.

So all the animals set off for the house under the tree root at the edge of the forest where Goblin lived. He was excited, too, because it was Christmas Eve.

"Hello, Goblin. There's a pair of slippers in the forest and we wondered if they would fit you."

Since the snow was so deep the deer let Goblin ride on his back. They soon found the slippers again but, when Goblin tried them on, they were far too big.

Now what? They could not just leave the slippers lying in the snow.

"I know," said Goblin. "There's an old woman who lives not far from here. If we took them to her I'm sure she would be glad of them."

"What a good idea!" said all the animals and off they went with the fox carrying one slipper and the squirrel the other.

It was hard work carrying them through the deep snow but at last they reached the old woman's cottage. There was a light in the window so they put the slippers down on the doorstep and then hid.

The old woman heard some strange rustling and pattering sounds outside and opened her door to see what was going on.

"Well I never!" she said in surprise as she picked up the slippers. "Fancy that! What beautiful slippers!"

The animals and Goblin held their breath as she went back into her cottage with the new slippers and shaking her head in a puzzled fashion.

"That was a good idea of yours, Goblin," they all said when she had shut her door and then they crept up and peeped in the window and saw that the slippers fitted as if they had been made for her.

On their way home the animals met Santa Claus returning from delivering his presents. They had all been given away and his sack was quite empty.

"Never mind," said Hoppy. "We found a lot of nice things lying in the snow a little while ago. You did mean them for us, didn't you?"

Santa Claus smiled. He had noticed the hole in his sack. Well, at least he knew where the things had gone now.

"And we gave the slippers to the old woman in the cottage," added Goblin and Santa Claus was very pleased to hear that because he had been going to take the slippers to her anyway!

"If you are all so good at giving presents," he said wearily, "you can help me next year and then I will not be as tired as I am today."

"Of course we'll help you," said the animals happily. "Goodbye, Santa, until next year," and they all ran off merrily to Goblin's house.

When they got there they could hardly believe their eyes.

There was a beautifully decorated Christmas tree outside the little house under the tree root with a manger for the animals and a bird table beside it.

"Oh, how lovely!" cried Goblin. "Now we can all have a Christmas party together!"

The animals were delighted and stood around the Christmas tree with its bright candles and felt happier than they had ever done in their lives.

"Living in the forest is nice," smiled Goblin looking lovingly at his friends.

Everyone was quiet and full of awe and their eyes shone as they enjoyed their feast.

"But Christmas in the forest is best of all," he added.

"Where's the little deer?" asked Hoppy looking round suddenly.

"Ssh!" said Squeaker. "He's gone to sleep over there."

And, of course, he was having sweet dreams.

Santa's Surprises

Written by Maggie Kay
Illustrated by John Geering

Santa's Surprises

The fairies and elves were enjoying their Christmas party when Santa Claus finished work. The tired, old man heard the sound of their laughter and music as he led his sleepy reindeer to the barn for a well-earned rest. He smiled and said,

"Well done, boys! Thank you." as the deer snuggled down in the straw.

Meanwhile, the fairies and elves were playing musical statues. They had to dance around the room and then, when the music stopped, they had to hold the position they were in and stand as still as they possibly could. Anyone who moved was out and the last one in was the winner.

The music stopped and - bump! - Holly, the fairy, fell to the floor in a heap and everyone burst out laughing. She had been flying and, when she stopped flapping her wings, pretending to be a statue, she had fallen, of course.

Embarrassed, she crept outside and, seeing Santa's sleigh by the barn decided to invite him to the party.

Inside the barn Holly found Santa fast asleep and giggled as she heard him snoring but, suddenly, she felt sorry for him.

"He must be worn out after travelling all over the world to make Christmas wonderful for all the children," she thought, "and now he's too tired to enjoy Christmas himself. What a shame!"

Holly flapped her wings and flew back to the party. Everyone was sitting at a big table tucking into fairy cakes, trifles, ice cream and jelly. One naughty elf threw some jelly across the table at another elf. Splat! It hit Eddie Elf in the face.

"Stop that, Elmer," said Holly, surprising the naughty elf by tapping him on the head as she flew over him.

Holly found her place at the table next to Ivy, Queen of the Christmas fairies, and said to her,

"Santa's asleep in the barn. I feel so sad. I've never even thought how tired he must be after making all the boys and girls happy and yet no-one gives him anything. He makes Christmas special but where are his presents? Maybe we could find some for him before he wakes up."

"Yes! You're right. Christmas should be special for Santa too," said Ivy and she banged on the table. "Listen, everyone, listen. Poor Santa is fast asleep and tired out in the barn and so he won't enjoy Christmas and he won't even have any presents to open. Let's all think and see what we can do to make Christmas special for Santa because he works so hard for everyone else."

After a few moments a group of fairies suggested spinning a silken cover to put over Santa to keep him warm in the barn.

"Good idea," said Ivy nodding her approval. "Set to work straight away."

Eddie and Elmer prepared a delicous meal ready for when Santa woke up and put it by him in the barn. Other elves and fairies made surprise presents of all shapes and sizes for Santa.

In the morning Santa still lay sleeping on the straw but, now, he was covered with the silken spread. A big meal and a huge pile of presents awaited him but Santa slept all day . . . and the next day . . . and the next.

Santa's food was replaced each day. Everyone kept thinking of new presents to bring him and soon the barn was full.

"Whatever are we going to do with all these presents?" Holly asked Ivy. "Christmas is over."

"I think I know," answered Ivy. "Children open a little window in an Advent calendar every day in December leading up to Christmas, don't they? They get a surprise every day."

"Mmmm," agreed a puzzled Holly.

"Well," said Ivy, "we have enough presents to give him a surprise each day till next Christmas."

"What a wonderful idea!" gasped Holly.

While Santa slept, the elves and fairies took all the parcels from the barn to Queen Ivy's castle. It was hard work trudging to and from the castle.

No sooner had the last parcel been taken away than Santa began to stir. Holly and Ivy watched as he yawned, sat up, stretched and then noticed the lovely silken spread on his lap.

"For me? What a lovely surprise," he smiled.

Every morning after that, until the following Christmas, there was a special surprise for Santa on his doorstep.

Sometimes it was a carving from a carpenter elf, sometimes socks, or a pretty lampshade, or a jar of honey, or sweets, or pyjamas.

As Christmas drew near again, the surprises were a new, red hat, black boots, a string of bells and a new, red suit.

So Santa enjoyed a whole wonderful year of surprises.

Ben Behaving Badly

Written by Maggie Kay
Illustrated by John Geering

Ben Behaving Badly

The fairies flitted round from house to house checking that the children were being good boys and girls. It was their duty to report to Santa Claus if anyone was naughty and did not deserve a Christmas present.

Fairy Floss peeped through the curtains at Number 3, Sunnyside Street. Yes, all was well there. Bea was helping her mummy bath her baby sister so Fairy Floss marked a tick on a little report sheet where it said, 'Bea at Number 3'.

Next she flew on to Number 5. As the letter-box flapped in the wind, Fairy Floss saw Clive help his mummy tidy up his toys and put them in the toybox. Fairy Floss added a tick to her report beside, 'Clive at Number 5'.

At Number 7, however, Fairy Floss could not decide. As she watched through the window, Kevin was having a temper tantrum. He stamped his foot and shouted "No!" when his daddy told him to eat his tea. Then he knocked his mug of milk to the floor.

"Oh dear," sighed Fairy Floss. "Kevin isn't behaving very well at all tonight."

Just as she was about to put a cross on her report sheet where it said, 'Kevin at Number 7', Kevin threw his arms around his daddy's neck and said,

"Sorry, Daddy."

Fairy Floss decided to give Kevin another chance and wrote a tick instead of a cross. She was a kind lady and hated to see children sad or disappointed at Christmas.

When she had finished all the odd numbers in the street, Fairy Floss flew over the road to meet Fairy Fran who was checking on the children in the houses with even numbers.

Kate at Number 8 was being very sweet. She was ready for bed, clutching her teddy and teaching him to say his prayers.

Fairy Fran ticked her report sheet next to, 'Kate at Number 8'

But, at Number 10, Ben was behaving badly. He pulled the puppy's tail, took his brother's toys and tugged the needles from the jumper Granny was knitting - all while Granny was not looking.

The puppy yelped, Ben's brother yelled and Granny was very cross when she saw her unravelled knitting.

"Wasn't me," fibbed Ben when Granny scolded him.

As Fairy Fran sadly marked a big cross on the report sheet where it said, 'Ben at Number 10', Elmer Elf came along asking what was wrong and Fairy Fran explained how naughty Ben was being.

"It's not good enough," she cried, "especially so close to Christmas."

"If he's naughty tomorrow then I'll visit him instead of Santa," said Elmer.

"Oh no!" gasped Fairy Floss and her face turned white with dread as she thought of the stories she had heard about Elmer Elf visiting bad boys and girls at Christmas. He left stones wrapped in Christmas paper and nasty cough sweets.

"Please give Ben another chance," pleaded Fairy Floss. "He can't be naughty always."

She could not sleep that night for thinking of Ben waking up on Christmas morning and opening his presents - only to find stones.

"Poor little boy," she thought. "I must help him to behave. Tomorrow is his last chance."

She decided to visit Ben there and then. She put on her cosy, fur-trimmed cape and flew to Number 10, Sunnyside Street. There, she gently squeezed through the letterbox, surprising the sleeping puppy as she fluttered past him on her way up the stairs. The puppy blinked and then fell asleep again.

Ben and his brother were fast asleep in bunk beds. Fairy Floss saw Ben on the top bunk and flew up to his pillow.

She pulled a tiny flute from her belt and played soothing music into Ben's ear. Every so often she stopped playing and whispered to Ben to be good. Then she sprinkled some magic dust over him before setting off for home.

On Christmas Eve, Fairy Floss checked the children in the houses with odd numbers and every child got a tick for being good.

When she met Fairy Fran, she asked her how Ben at Number 10 had behaved.

"You'll never believe it! It's like magic!" Fairy Fran exclaimed. "All day Ben has behaved like a little angel. I've given him a gold star."

Fairy Floss was glad. She knew that the gold star would cancel out any crosses.

After Santa had called on the children, she made another round of Sunnyside Street, peeping through the windows.

There was Bea at Number 3, Clive at Number 5, Kevin at Number 7 and Ben at Number 10 - all playing happily with their wonderful new toys.

"Merry Christmas, everyone!" whispered Fairy Floss.

The Christmas Wish

Written by Maggie Kay
Illustrated by John Geering

The Christmas Wish

Paul and his daddy were sledging in the park. Wheee! Paul loved zooming down the hill.

"One more time please, Daddy," he cried when Daddy said it was time to go.

"Okay, but this is definitely the last," smiled Daddy.

Paul shot down the slope and then slid slowly to a halt. He was just about to beg Daddy to let him have another go when something caught his eye.

It was Paul's favourite thing. It was fluffy and bouncy and wet and excited. It was Uncle Peter's puppy.

"Patch," called Paul, running from his sledge.

Uncle Peter unleashed Patch and the puppy bounded towards Paul. It leapt up on him, bowling him over. Paul wrapped his arms around the puppy and soon they were both rolling about in the snow.

Next they played hide and seek through the shrubs and Paul chuckled at the puppy's tell-tale paw prints in the snow.

"Not long now till Christmas," Uncle Peter said to Paul. "What are you going to ask Santa Claus to bring you?"

"A puppy!" Paul replied quickly.

"You can't have a puppy, Paul," Daddy said gently. "There isn't room in our flat."

Paul dropped his head so no-one would see his tears. He wanted a puppy more than anything in the world.

Back home, Mummy asked Paul if he would like to stir the Christmas pudding.

"Make a wish as you stir it," she told him, giving him a wooden spoon.

"I wish I could have a . . . ," began Paul.

"Don't say it aloud," cried Mummy. "It has to be a secret or your wish won't come true."

Paul closed his eyes and made his wish as he stirred the Christmas pudding.

The next week, Mummy and Daddy took Paul to the huge toy store in town. It was packed full of people and had every toy you could imagine.

Whenever Paul stopped to look at something, Daddy would say,

"Why don't you ask Santa to bring you that?"

Mummy suggested a computer but Paul just shook his head.

A puppy was the only thing he wanted.

As Christmas grew nearer, the children at Paul's nursery class got more and more excited but Paul became quieter than usual. He refused to go to the nursery Christmas party and, when Daddy offered to help him to write a note to Santa Claus, Paul said that it did not matter. If he could not have a puppy, he did not want anything. He was a sad, little boy.

On Christmas Eve, when Paul was asleep, Mummy said to Daddy,

"I wish we had let Paul have a puppy. I hate to see him so sad."

"Me too," agreed Daddy.

Now, like all boys and girls, Paul had a fairy godmother who looked after him. He did not know, of course, because she was invisible to children. Her name was Dogma and she was a jolly, little lady who liked to see her children happy. She was in a tizzy over Paul.

"The only thing to make him happy is a puppy," she sighed, "but his mummy and daddy say he can't have one. What am I to do?"

As she paced backward and forward along the street where Paul lived, she heard a funny sound. She stopped to listen. The noise came again from a shop doorway. Inside the doorway was a shopping bag and inside the bag was - a puppy wrapped in rags.

The puppy looked at Dogma with sad, appealing eyes.

"You poor thing," said the fairy godmother. "You've been abandoned! I know a little boy who would love to look after you! Oh, but there's a problem . . .," she thought, remembering about Paul's mummy and daddy.

When the tiny puppy shivered and whimpered, Dogma decided to take a chance.

She stuck a Christmas label on the shopping bag saying *"For Paul Happy Christmas."* Then, when Santa came, she popped the bag on to his sleigh, next to Paul's other presents.

Paul stirred in his sleep as the puppy let out a little yelp but, when the puppy barked, Paul sat bolt upright in his bed!

"Santa's brought me a puppy!" he yelled.

FOR PAUL
HAPPY
CHRISTMAS!

Mummy and Daddy rushed through to Paul's room, surprised to see the puppy.

"My wish came true!" called Paul.

"Mine too," laughed Mummy, pleased to see Paul happy again.

"I'll call you Rags," Paul told the puppy and Rags barked as if to say "Okay".

Neither of them was aware of their fairy godmother (or should that be dogmother?) as Dogma peeped through the window at the happy scene. She was pleased she had done the right thing.

Santa's Lucky Star

Written and Illustrated
by John Geering

Santa's Lucky Star

"Oh dear me!" said Santa to himself, as he looked at his reindeer who were all in their beds, coughing and sneezing with colds. "The poor things will not be able to pull my sleigh tonight. What will I do?"

He stood outside, next to the sleigh, all filled up with presents for the children, and he looked up at a bright star.

"I suppose I could make a wish on a lucky star. That might help." So he did.

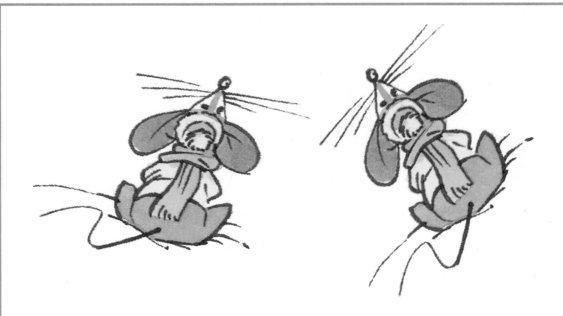

Santa had no sooner finished making his wish,
when, to his surprise, the bright star got bigger and
bigger and bigger. It landed a few feet from him.
glowing brightly.

"Gracious me!" was all Santa could say.

He was almost blinded by the bright light and
then a voice came from the star.

"Hello! Can I help you?" said the voice.

"Goodness me and gracious me again!"
spluttered the very startled Santa.

The bright light dimmed and Santa could see a small space-craft. He had never seen anything like it before. It was silver, just like a star, with flashing, coloured lights. A hatch opened at the top and a cute, funny, little Alien popped his head out and grinned at Santa.

"I'm Fred, from the Red Planet. I will pull your sleigh tonight."

"Well I never," gasped Santa, more surprised than ever.

Within minutes, Santa's sleigh was hitched up to the space-craft. Santa sat in the sleigh and Fred, the Alien, waved to him from the hatch.

"Hold on to your hat! Here we go!"

Whoosh! The space-craft took to the air pulling Santa and his sleigh faster than he had ever travelled before.

"Holly and Ivy!" exclaimed Santa. "At this rate I'll be back before I've started."

They sped swiftly and silently through the night sky, darting this way and that to avoid trees, tall buildings and chimneys. They hovered by the chimney stacks while Santa delivered the presents then, swoosh, on to the next town. They flew over land and sea, forests and towns, high over mountains and low into valleys to the tiniest of villages. No child was left out. Then they flew home.

"Well!" thought Santa. "That was the fastest trip on record without a doubt." Then he and Fred, the Alien, sat down at the table in Santa's cosy cottage to a hot drink and a large piece of Christmas cake served up by the kitchen gnome.

Then Santa saw a big tear roll down the Alien's cheek and plop on to the table.

"Oh dear! What's the matter?" asked Santa kindly and Fred looked up at him and, choking back the tears, said,

"I'm lost. I can't find my way home."

Santa took his sack and dug deep into it. He pulled out a brightly-wrapped parcel and handed it to Fred.

"I almost forgot to give you your present, Fred. Go on, open it."

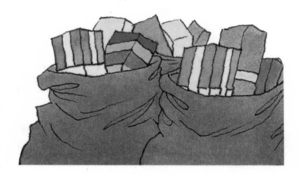

Beaming, Fred took the present and began to open it carefully. His eyes lit up when he saw what it was - a big book entitled *The Tourists' Guide to the Universe*.

"Just what I needed!" shouted the excited Fred. "Now I can find my way home!"

Santa waved Fred off as he and his little space-craft zoomed off into the Christmas sky.

"You are a star, Fred, my lucky star," called Santa after him. "A Happy Christmas to everyone on your planet."

Fred looked back at Santa, grinning a happy Christmas grin and waving. He called,

"See you again, Santa. A Happy Christmas to everyone!"

So - next time you see a big, bright star in the sky, twinkling at you, call out,

"Hello!"

You never know! It might just be Fred.

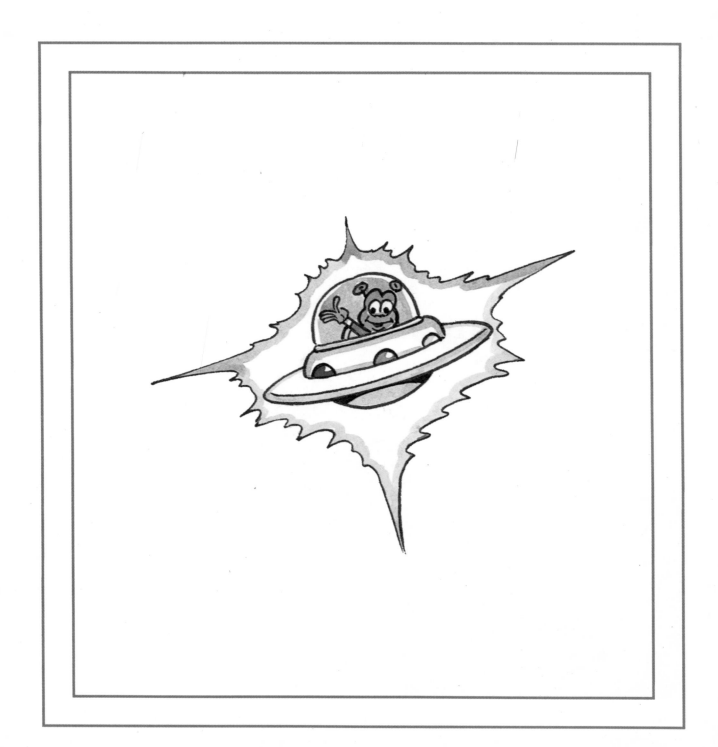

THE END

CONTENTS